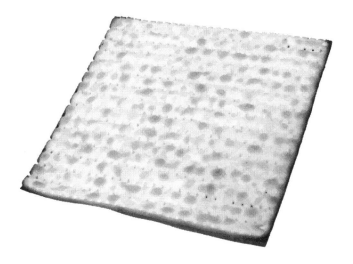

Also by Izzy Abrahmson

The Village Life Series
A Village Romance
Winter Blessings
The Village Twins
The Village Feasts
The Council of Wise Women (Soon…)

As Mark Binder
Fictions
The Groston Rules
*A Dead Politician, an Undead Clam,
and an Ancient Horror*
Loki Ragnarok
It Ate My Sister
The Zombie Cat
The Rationalization Diet

Stories for young people
Cinderella Spinderella
The Bed Time Story Book
Kings, Wolves, Princesses and Lions
Genies, Giants and a Walrus
Classic Stories for Boys and Girls
Tall Tales, Whoppers and Lies
It was a dark and stormy night…
Stories for Peace
Transmit Joy!

THE VILLAGE FEASTS

Izzy Abrahmson

Light Publications
Providence

Design by Lou Pop

Thanks to all my readers and listeners, especially Jim Rosenberg,
Vida Hellman, Ida and Steve Colchamiro, Rose Pavlow, Navah Levine,
and of course Harry, Francesca, Max, and Elaine K. Binder. Thanks to
Jessica Everette and Nina Rooks Cast for their support and proofreading,
and to Sara deBeer and Michael Okeke for their audiobook proofing.

Thanks to Fishel Bresler for his lovely music in the audiobook edition, to
Barry Dolinger for the lesson on how to bake matzah,
and to the Rhode Island Bureau of Jewish Education for the graphics.

Another version of "Mrs. Chaipul's Lead Sinker Matzah Balls" appears in
"A Village Romance" Stories in this collection have appeared in: *Cricket
Magazine, The Jewish Daily Forward, Washington Jewish Week, The Shofar,
Being Jewish, The Observer, American Jewish World, The Jewish Chronicle,
Jewish Western Bulletin, The Jewish Journal, Arizona Jewish Post, Greater
Phoenix Jewish News, Chicago JUF News, Chicago Jewish Star, Charlotte
Jewish News, American Jewish World, Jewish Free Press, The Chelmsford
Independent, The Jewish Advocate & Jewish Times, Ohio Jewish Chronicle,
The Wisconsin Jewish Chronicle, The School Magazine...*

Softcover ISBN: 978-1-940060-45-3
eBook ISBN: 978-1-940060-50-7
Audiobook ISBN: 978-1-940060-55-2
Library of Congress Control Number: 2021937779

Printed in the United States of America
10 9 8 7 6 5 4 3 2 1

Light Publications
PO Box 2462
Providence, RI 02906
U. S. A.
www.lightpublications.com

Have an excellent day!

Contents

Foreword.. 3
Chiri Bim / Chiri Bom?........................... 5
Mega Matzah Mishugas.......................... 11
Mrs. Chaipul's Lead Sinker Matzah Balls...... 21
Knock Knock.. 31
Cabbage Matzah 39
The Seder Switch 47
By the Book.. 55
Temptation 63
Home is Where the Seder Is 71
The Village Will Not Go Hungry 79
Author's Note... 87
A Village Glossary................................... 89
About the Author 96
The Village Life Series.............................. 98
The Village Life Podcast........................... 99

For our families –
all the Binders, Delaneys,
Brennans, Colchamiros, Aarons,
Hagens, Kotells, Berlowe-Binders,
and of course the Abrahmsons

Foreword

Welcome to Chelm! Welcome to the village of fools. Eighty households and farms, a few dirt roads, more chickens than people, and a wealth of love, lore, misadventures and often silliness.

You may wonder, where exactly is Chelm? It's not that no one knows, it's just hard to explain. On the edge of the Black Forest, somewhere between Russia and Poland, and occasionally Germany. If you travel through the town of Smyrna chances are good you'll get lost, and maybe end up in the village of Chelm.

There, you will rub elbows with Reb Stein the baker, the Gold family, Doodle the orphan, Rabbi Kibbitz and Mrs. Chaipul, and of course, the Schlemiels.

Winters are hard in Chelm, and the eight days of Passover mark the transition between dark icy cold and the warm sunshine. The streets turn to mud, the weather is inconsistent, and for a whole week you're not allowed to eat bread, only matzah. This is never easy, and so the villagers do their best to laugh and smile and complain, while they gather together to celebrate and break bread.

Okay the bread is still matzah, made with nothing but flour and water. No salt. No yeast. You would think it would be tasteless, but it's not. It's crisp and light and filling.

And when you do break matzah with friends and family it doesn't smoosh or rip or tear. Matzah snaps with a satisfyingly sharp crack.

Chiri Bim / Chiri Bom?

A nigun is a tune with words of nonsense.
This famous one originated in The Village…

Many years ago, in the village of Chelm there were two families, the Chiribim and the Chiribom. They were enemies. They fought over everything. They fought over land, they fought over water, they fought over cows and horses and chickens. They fought over air.

The Chiribim and Chiribom didn't talk to each other. They were stubborn. They didn't look at each other.

In the synagogue and village hall, they would sit on opposite sides of the room and glare or shout or scream. Or spit. It was disgusting.

The feud had been going on for years, decades, perhaps centuries. No one knew where it began or how it had originated. What insult had provoked the first Chiribim to scorn the first Chiribom? It was long ago and long forgotten.

Sometimes the anger came to blows, but fortunately so far no one had been seriously injured or killed.

Rabbi Kibbitz, the oldest and wisest of leaders, was sick of it. He was tired of the malice, tired of the hatred, tired of the tension. He was tired of mopping spit off the floor of the synagogue.

So he decided to solve the problem. The Chiribim and Chiribom needed to come together to work out their differences. They were farmers, they worked the land. They were neighbors, living so close to each other but so far away.

The problem was that he couldn't get them all in the same room without someone blowing up.

It had been pouring rain for most of the week of Passover, and everyone was cranky.

In those days, after a long rain, everyone in the village would go out into the woods to pick mushrooms. Mothers, fathers, grandmothers, grandfathers, aunts, uncles, cousins, brothers and sisters would all pack up their lunches, bring along empty baskets, and hunt for wild treasure. The youngsters would find dozens of kinds of fungi, and the elders would teach them which ones were tasty, which were revolting, and which might kill you.

During the rainstorm, Rabbi Kibbitz sent a note to the Chiribim asking them to join him in the forest for lunch. He also sent a note to the Chiribom asking them to join him for lunch in the same place, at the same time.

Early the next morning, the rabbi pulled on his boots, put a basket over his arm and plodded into the Black Forest. First he would find the Chiribim and then the Chiribom. And then they would work it all out.

Unfortunately, he forgot his glasses, so he was having a hard time seeing where he was going.

Soon, he came upon a group of people.

"Chiribim?" he asked them.

They shook their heads. "Chiribom," they answered.

Sighing, the Rabbi continued his search.

He realized he should change his tactics. He would meet with the Chiribom first, and then the Chiribim.

Soon, he came upon another group of people. "Chiribom?" he asked them.

They shrugged, "Chiribim."

"Hmmm." The rabbi wandered off, muttering, "Chiribim Bom Bim Bom Bim Bom"

Another group of people were asked, "Chiribom?" and they answered, "Chiribim."

The next group were queried, "Chiribim?" and they replied "Chiribom."

The rabbi was getting frustrated. "Ai Chiribiri biri bim bom bom, Ai Chiri biri biri bim bom bom."

Back and forth the rabbi went racing through the forest. If he asked, "Chiribim?" they told him, "Chiribom." If he asked "Chiribom," they told him, "Chiribim."

"Ai Chiri biri biri bim bom bom. Ai Chiri biri biri bom."

The Chiribim and Chiribom were stubborn. They loved an argument, and neither group liked to be pinned down or admit to anything. Perhaps they were playing tricks on the rabbi. Perhaps they were just being obstinate.

"Bim!" the rabbi shouted.

"Bom!" they answered.

"Bom?" the rabbi yelped.

"Bim!" came a chorus.

"AAAGH! Bimbom Bimbom Bimbom!"

He began to twirl about.

He asked another group, "Bom?"

They answered, "Bim!"

The next had to be… "Bom?"

"Nu. Bim!"

"Impossible! Bimbom Bimbom Bimbom!"

The rabbi was running and twirling, almost dancing. "Ai Chiribiri biri bim bom bom."

His hair was everywhere. His coat was open. "Ai Chiri biri biri bim bom bom. Ai Chiri biri biri bim bom bom. Ai Chiri biri biri bom."

Well, the Chiribim and the Chiribom started laughing. They couldn't help themselves. Their rabbi, this wise old man, was acting like a chicken with his head cut off, like a frog trying to escape a pack of curious boys, like a school teacher with a cube of ice dropped down his back. All the time he was muttering to himself like a crazy man, "Chiribimbombimbombimbom."

They laughed, and they grinned, and they smiled, and then they looked up.

Across the forest they saw something that they had never seen before.

They saw each other smiling and laughing and grinning.

They looked and they realized that they all wore the same kind of clothes. They had the same kinds of shoes and hats and hair. They all held baskets full of mushrooms.

So the Chiribim and the Chiribom came together in the middle of the forest, and shook hands, and they kissed cheeks, and they hugged.

And of course they had a Passover lunch.

Such a feast! Chopped liver on matzah with fresh-picked mushrooms. Beet salad. Brisket. And Mrs. Chaipul's light as a feather lemon meringue pie. So delicious!

When they were done eating and finished cleaning up, they lifted the poor rabbi up on their shoulders, because he was still too dizzy to walk, and all together they carried him back to the village of Chelm, singing:

"Ai Chiri biri biri bim bom bom…"

From that day on they were no longer known as the Chiribim or the Chiribom, but as the Chiribimbombimbombimbom…. Bim… Bom.

Ai Chiri biri biri bim bom bom.
Ai Chiri biri biri bim bom bom.
Ai Chiri biri biri bom…

Mega Matzah Mishugas

Once, many many years ago in the village of Chelm, a disaster struck right in the middle of the Passover Seder. There was chaos, food flew through the air, children ran shrieking to their mothers....

But wait, it is important that you understand a few details.

First, you should know that Reb Stein, the baker of Chelm, was the earliest inventor of the thin cracker-like matzah that we know today.

Traditionally, matzah in Chelm, and everywhere else in the world, had been a rather thick piece of something bread-like or pancakesque, usually round, always flat, and incredibly chewy that got stale fast.

Experimenting with his recipe, Reb Stein accidentally heated his ovens too much and made his dough too thin.

The results were initially disheartening.

These things were crisp to the point of brittle, and looked a little like tan-colored shingles that you might put on a roof.

Rather than throw the batch out, he stacked them in the corner, which was fortunate because when the oven broke later that week, and everyone in Chelm was clamoring for their Passover matzah, the new matzahs weren't moldy, and Reb Stein was still able to supply the villagers.

"But is it Kosher for Passover?" Rabbi Kibbitz asked Rabbi Yohon Abrahms, who was both the school teacher and the mashgiach responsible for making sure that everything was kosher.

"Yesh," declared Rabbi Abrams, his mouth full of the new matzah shmeared with chopped liver. "And tasty, too!"

So, from that year on, Reb Stein's matzah was baked crunchy.

The next thing you should know, for the purpose of this particular tale, is that every year, weather permitting – which in Chelm was not very often – all the villagers gathered in the round square outside the synagogue to celebrate a communal Pesach feast. It was a potluck affair, with each family of Chelm contributing some portion of the meal.

Rabbi Kibbitz supplied the blessings. Mrs. Chaipul would bring her famous lead-ball knaidlach soup. Reb Cantor prepared gallons of kosher l'Pesach homemade wine, and poured hundreds of cups, at least four per person (with kosher grape juice for the youngsters). The Levitzkys, Mrs. and Reb, worked together and dazzled everyone's sweet tooth with their mysterious chopped apple Sephardic charoses.

And, every year, the baker, Reb Stein, baked his special crisp flat matzah for all of Chelm.

This particular year, however, Reb Stein had a goal. He had decided to create the world's largest matzah.

Now, in the past, one of the czars, Fyodor, The Not So Great, had commissioned, from the bakers in Moscow, an unleavened bread the size of a tabletop. Jews in London had once witnessed a *hamotzi* over a matzah as big as a horse cart. And it was rumored that in Jerusalem bakers had been developing for centuries a secret recipe that they claimed would permit them to rebuild the

Holy Temple completely out of matzah within a week, if the Messiah should ever come and call for it.

Given such stiff competition, Rabbi Yohon Abrahms argued that Reb Stein could never hope to compete.

"Chelm is such a small village," Rabbi Abrahms said. "What do we need with something so big? Be careful that you don't call down the wrath of the Almighty for your arrogance."

"Phooey," said Reb Stein. "I will be written into the *Gibberish Book of World Records*, alongside the man with the largest inflamed toe."

Before entering his chametz-free workshop, with its huge brick oven, Reb Stein would wash, change his clothes, and put on gloves and a veil, like a bride, to prevent contamination. For weeks he slaved, "Like our forefathers in Egypt," he claimed. His eyes took on a burning look, or perhaps it was just the singes on his eyebrows from the intense heat.

There were hundreds of rejects, broken scraps of matzah that looked like blackened shingles, and tasted like unsalted tree bark.

So, on the day before Pesach, with none of their individual matzah orders filled yet, the citizens were both curious, and concerned about the progress of their baker.

"I hear", said Reb Gold the cobbler, "that if he fails, he'll shoot himself."

"Oh, that would be bad," said Joseph Katz, "because he still owes me money from our *Chanukah dreidel* game."

"You'd better talk to him now," said Reb Gold. "The man is close to madness."

But just then, Joel Cantor, Reb Cantor's youngest son, ran up and breathlessly announced, "Reb Stein has made the biggest matzah in the world!"

"Well, good," said a relieved Joseph Katz, "I'll still make sure I collect after the Seder."

Just then, from around the corner, with a clatter of hoofbeats, came Reb Stein, dressed elegantly in white. He drove a team of six horses struggling to pull three wagons lashed together!

Everyone craned their necks for a look, but the Mega-Matzah was hidden from sight by a huge matzah cover made from fourteen bed sheets borrowed, after a ferocious argument, from Mrs. Stein's linen closet.

"Tomorrow night!" Reb Stein laughed, as he rode his wagons into the round village square. "Tomorrow night, you will all see, and admire!"

"He sounds sick," said Reb Gold.

"He needs help," agreed Joseph Katz.

All through the Seder, the citizens stared at the Mega Matzah's cover.

It was so gigantic! It had been moved off the wagons, and now four whole banquet tables were devoted to supporting it. The men who had moved it from the wagons to the tables said that it weighed more than all of Mrs. Chaipul's cast-iron knaidels put together! (And that was something!)

After the four questions, and following the *hamotzi*, Rabbi Kibbitz turned to Reb Stein, who waved away Rabbi Yohon Abrahms.

"Not yet!" said Reb Stein. "I made a special, smaller matzah. To keep the suspense."

This was a fortunate thing, because the man from the *Gibberish Book of World Records* was late.

Reb Stein was nervous, and kept looking over his shoulder. Before it was devoured, his creation needed to be witnessed and documented!

Rabbi Yohon Abrahms, not very helpfully, giggled as he peeked under the matzah covers and brought out a matzah that was the size of a window!

This Mini-Mega-Matzah was not gargantuan, but it tasted fine.

The meal began, and with the help of several cups of Reb Cantor's wine, the villagers finally managed to choke down Mrs. Chaipul's shot put knaidel's, and thoroughly enjoyed the rest of the huge feast and service.

At last, it was time for dessert, and for Reb Stein to unveil his masterpiece!

Reb Stein rose from his seat of honor, and scanned the village's round square for any sign of the record-keeper from the *Gibberish Book*. If the man didn't show up soon, the ambitious baker's hopes would be dashed and his masterpiece digested.

Fortunately for Reb Stein's ulcer, a horse carriage pulled into the small village, drove past the Yeshiva, and stopped at the edge of the feast. An old man peered out from the carriage's window at the four covered tables.

Reb Stein grinned, grasped the matzah cover, and with a grand flourish (tugging several times because Mrs. Stein's sheets were so heavy) revealed…

Not a mammoth monumental matzah. Not a world record sized giant cracker. Not even a humongous piece of unleavened bread.

What the people of Chelm saw before them was large. It was huge. It was flat. It was black.

It was a roof.

(Yes, a roof, with shingles and all.)

As one person, the villagers of Chelm gasped.

This was the moment that the *mishugas* mentioned at the beginning of this story began...

There was chaos, leftover food flew through the air, and children ran shrieking to their mothers.

Reb Stein, his ulcer forgotten, clutched at his heart. The man from *Gibberish* shook his head sadly, pulled the drapes of his horse carriage shut, and ordered his driver to leave.

You wouldn't have thought that such disappointment would cause anyone amusement, but just then, Rabbi Yohon Abrahms and ten of his Yeshiva students fell out of their chairs with laughter!

In the dead of night, Rabbi Abrahms explained between guffaws, he and his students had switched the Mega-Matzah with the roof from the Yeshiva science laboratory. And now, the matzah was on the roof, and the roof was on the matzah tables.

All the citizens of Chelm ran to the school. The horse carriage from *Gibberish* was just ahead of them, about to leave Chelm forever.

Reb Stein gasped as he saw his masterpiece of white and brown, perfectly baked unleavened bread suspended high on top of the walls of the place of learning.

"Wait!" shouted Reb Stein. "Wait! Look at the size of it!" He jumped up and down and waved for the official in the carriage to come back.

But by then the carriage was long gone, and with it went Reb Stein's chance at record-making history.

After not so long, some impatient children suggested that it was still time for dessert, so Rabbi Abrahms and his Yeshiva students, with their backs straining, took the Mega-Matzah off the roof and returned it to the Seder.

While Reb Stein sobbed and cursed, the huge afikomen – which almost certainly would have broken the record – was broken up into large plate-sized pieces, and eaten with appetites whetted by laughter. This one was even more delicious than the first. Everyone said, "What a wonderful thing Reb Stein has done!"

(Not to mention that, when the meal was concluded, there was more than enough unleavened bread left over to feed the entire village for the entire week of Passover.)

They say that Reb Stein, although he still bakes the best matzah in the world, has never quite recovered. And he does take some small revenge. From that day to this, year-round, every cake, *challah*, biscuit and bread that he sells to his friend Rabbi Abrahms is as flat as a matzah.

Rabbi Abrahms doesn't complain, though; he trusts that some day, with the help of the Almighty, he'll get another rise out of Reb Stein.

Mrs. Chaipul's Lead Sinker Matzah Balls

So, what's the story with Mrs. Chaipul's Matzah balls?

Mrs. Chaipul is a wonderful cook. When you run the only kosher restaurant in the village of Chelm, you have to be. Her *kugel* is incredible; her *kreplach* are tender and moist; her corned beef and cabbage melt in your mouth; her roasted potatoes are hot and crisp; and her split pea soup is so rich and robust, you'd swear it was *treif*. Even her potato latkes, which were once the scourge of Chanukah, have improved greatly over the past few years—that is another story.

But her lead sinker matzah balls will never change. This is the story of those matzah balls—and how they saved the village.

When Mrs. Chaipul first moved to Chelm, she brought her matzah ball recipe with her. It had been in her family for generations, passed down in secret from mother to daughter.

In the Chaipul family, jaw-breaking matzah balls were an immutable tradition, like plucking a chicken on the first day of spring. Every year, the Chaipul men joked that the secret was building construction mortar—a comment that was met with stony silence by the women. At one Seder, Mrs. Chaipul's grandfather Moishe had argued for six hours that if the pyramids in Egypt had only been built from his wife's matzah balls, then they would still be standing. Never mind that his son-in-law, Sam Klammerdinger (Mrs. Chaipul's first husband, may he rest in peace), tried to convince Moishe that the pyramids really were still standing. It was indisputable that, undigested, a Chaipul Knaidel could last for generations.

In Chelm, the villagers' first taste of the Chaipul Knaidel was the second year after she had opened the restaurant. The first year, Mrs. Chaipul was too busy to clean and make the facility kosher for Passover, so she shut down and arranged for a *goyishe* intermediary to buy the restaurant for the eight-day festival.

During that first Passover in Chelm, Mrs. Chaipul was invited to eat at the house of every villager. After all, with her shop closed, someone had to feed her.

Naturally she accepted Shoshana Cantor's invitation. Who wouldn't? Wasn't Reb Cantor the merchant the wealthiest man in Chelm? Wouldn't his Passover feast be the most sumptuous?

And it was. Mrs. Chaipul arrived well before sunset to find that all the work in the kitchen was done. Shoshana had servants to help her! When the table was set, it was beautiful. There were seven forks, three knives, and fourteen spoons. Mrs. Chaipul was at a loss to know where to begin. What did you do with seven forks except put them on the table, wash them and then put them back into the drawer?

Still, the *charoses* was tasty, with a hint of fresh orange from the Holy Land, and the matzah was Reb Stein the baker's finest *shmura*, round and crisp.

Then came the chicken soup, and for Mrs. Chaipul this was both a shock and a revelation. She looked at the walnut-sized matzah balls floating in the soup, and this in itself gave her pause. Floating matzah balls? She had never seen such a thing! She sighed, exercised her jaw a bit, lifted a knaidel with her spoon, and bit in.

When you're expecting to chew a rock and instead your teeth sink into lightly whipped air, it comes as something of a surprise. Her jaw dropped open as the matzah ball melted in her mouth. She sat there with the spoon held suspended in mid-air for quite some time.

"Is everything all right?" Shoshana Cantor asked. "Is there enough salt?"

Mrs. Chaipul realized that she was being rude, and she quickly closed her mouth. Her teeth cut through the matzah ball like a hot knife through butter. She chewed, and in seconds the matzah ball had dissolved as if it had never been.

"Interesting," she said quietly. And then she added, so as not to offend her hostess, "Quite tasty."

It was the same at every house she visited in Chelm. Far from being the stones of affliction, the matzah balls were soft, chewy, and, above all, edible.

By the end of Passover, Mrs. Chaipul was disheartened and confused. Had her family been doing something wrong for so many years? Or were the villagers of Chelm the misguided ones?

She took her concerns to Rabbi Kibbitz. This was in the days before they were married. In fact, it was one of the first private conferences that she and the learned man had. She explained her problem and waited for pearls of wisdom.

He was no help at all. "*Kabalah* I know," he said. "But cooking?" He shrugged. "I eat what's in front of me. Too much, if you ask some of the villagers." Then he laughed and patted his great stomach.

Mrs. Chaipul set the questions aside and went back to her restaurant.

A year passed, and once again Passover was fast approaching.

This year, Mrs. Chaipul was determined to be open for business, if not for the Seders, then for every other meal. She knew that most housewives only knew how to prepare matzah so many ways. She had in her possession the *Chaipul Pesach Cookbook*, which detailed more than fourteen hundred recipes made with matzah meal and potato starch alone and in combination.

Once again, she ate her Seder at the Cantor house and once again she was polite. This time, however, it was Reb Cantor who noticed her face.

"I understand that your restaurant will be open for Passover this year," he said. "Will you be making matzah ball soup?"

Mrs. Chaipul grinned. "Yes, of course. It wouldn't be Passover without the famous Chaipul Knaidel. I missed them last year and I thought I would give them away this year to make up for my mistake."

Reb Cantor's eyes widened. "You're giving away free food?!"

"Well," said Mrs. Chaipul with a shrug, "The matzah balls will be free, but the soup will still cost."

Reb Cantor smiled with understanding.

On the second day of Passover, despite the fact that it was pouring down rain, the line for Mrs. Chaipul's restaurant snaked out the door. She sent her customers home, wading back and forth through the muddy streets, to bring their kosher-for-Passover soup bowls so that she wouldn't have to spend the whole day and night washing dishes. Fortunately, she had anticipated the crowd, so she had made six kettles the size of washtubs full of matzah balls. Even so, she still wasn't sure there were going to be enough, so she had to set a limit of one per customer—at least until everyone had firsts.

She ladled soup and a knaidel into each bowl and said with a smile, "Remember that we were once slaves in Egypt."

The villagers thought this was interesting, and they were puzzled when the matzah ball sank to the bottom of the bowl with a clank.

Then they looked for a place to sit. The restaurant was crowded elbow to elbow, tighter than the shul for *Erev Kol Nidre*. The tables were full; the counter was packed. The children and young men were forced to slurp standing up, like wild animals.

Still the villagers felt jolly. Outside it was cold and wet and bucketing down rain. Inside Mrs. Chaipul's restaurant they were all warm and cozy, glowing with anticipation.

The soup was sweet and savory, rich with the snap of parsnip and perfectly peeled slices of carrot. It was, in the words of Rabbi Kibbitz, "Good enough to cure even an uncommon cold."

At last, it was time to eat the matzah balls.

These were bigger than those the villagers were accustomed to. Instead of the size of walnuts or chicken eggs, Mrs. Chaipul's matzah balls were as big as ripe apples. But you couldn't seem to cut them. And it wasn't so easy to get such a large knaidel into your mouth or even onto your spoon. They were so heavy that one child was forced to balance his bowl on his knees and use two hands to lift his.

At last came the bite, that first bite, the one that defines a matzah ball—and the matzah ball cook—forever.

Ow! It hurt. It wasn't so much hard like a rock, but it certainly was dense, like a clay brick before it has set in a mold. Your teeth could get into it, but it was hard work, like sawing wood with a nail file. After two minutes the villagers began to have second thoughts but found that their teeth had sunk in so deeply that they were trapped and there was no choice but to go on. After five minutes their jaws began to ache, and the villagers started to wonder whether Mrs. Chaipul's family had all died of lockjaw and starvation.

At last, one by one the villagers bit through with a sudden snap of tooth against tooth and were struck by the realization that they still had to chew the whole bite up because it would be rude and messy to spit it out onto the floor.

So chew they did. The afternoon dragged into evening. Rain was still pouring, and still they were chewing.

The flavor was sublime and robust, but it went on and on and on. Everyone nodded and smiled. Some mumbled, "*Goob!*" And then they chewed some more.

It was starting to get dark when, all of a sudden young Doodle, the village orphan, burst into the restaurant. He had forgotten that there was free food and had been wandering through the village looking for someone to tell his news.

"Mrs. Chaipul! Rabbi Kibbitz! The dam on the Bug River has burst! A flood is coming."

There wasn't time to think or plan. The villagers stampeded out of the restaurant, and ran to the banks of the river where the dam they had built years ago had finally broken.

A wall of water was rising up behind the dam. In minutes, it looked like the village of Chelm could be washed away and drowned, forgotten like the villages that Noah, from the safety of his ark, had watched vanish.

No one could speak—partly because they were in shock and partly because they were all still chewing. The villagers had been so upset, that they hadn't even bothered to put down their bowls and spoons.

Mrs. Chaipul, who had been too busy serving to eat a bite, broke the silence with a command.

"Throw your matzah balls into the river," she shouted. "Aim upstream from the break in the dam!"

The villagers did as they were told. Matzah balls went flying. More and more matzah balls flew into the river, landing with loud sploshes. They were caught by the current and wedged into the crack where they became lodged and stuck fast. Finally, the gap in the dam was sealed tight and not even a dribble leaked through.

Everyone wanted to cheer, but first they had to swallow, which they did, just as the rain stopped and the setting sun emerged from behind a cloud.

And then they cheered: "Mazel Tov for Mrs. Chaipul's Famous Knaidels!"

Mrs. Chaipul beamed and *kvelled*.

Then, much to her surprise, Rabbi Kibbitz kissed her on the cheek and whispered into her ear, "Delicious. You should never change that recipe."

What could she do? She didn't.

Knock Knock

About that evening I went missing, it isn't much of a story. The night was pitch black and I became completely lost. Fortunately, I found myself at the door to a small house. They must not have received many strangers in those parts, because every one in the village was soon jammed into that tiny room. I spun a yarn about a boy named Tom Sawyer and a dead cat, which they quite appreciated. Comedy, I suppose, being universal. The next day I managed to find my way back to my tour. Good soup with odd dumplings.
– From a letter by Samuel Clemens to Elisha Bliss, American Publishing Company.

The Seder was well under way at the home of Martin and Chaya Levitsky in the small village of Chelm. Since their children were grown and had gone off to seek their fortunes, and they only had young Doodle, the village orphan living in their house, it was the Levitsky's custom to invite their neighbors to share their Pesach feast. This year, they were celebrating with Joshua Gold, the cobbler, his wife Esther, and all their children. It was good to have so many young people in the house. Especially David Gold, who was a kind boy, and good friends with Doodle.

Dinner was long finished, and it was time at last to open the door for Elijah the Prophet. Reb Levitsky asked for volunteers.

David nudged Doodle, and Doodle nudged David. Both giggled. It was far past their bedtime, but neither would admit to being tired.

Reb Levitsky put on a stern face. "Someone must go. It would not do for the Messiah's herald to wait outside in the cold, and be forced to knock."

Just then there was a loud knocking at the door.

Everyone in the room jumped!

"What was that?" whispered Doodle.

"Maybe it's Elijah," David teased.

"Hush," warned Esther Gold. "Do not make such jokes."

All were quiet, listening.

"Just the wind," said Reb Gold. "You need to fix those window shutters, Martin."

"We don't have any shutters," said Reb Levitsky. "Perhaps we should open the door."

"I'm not going," said Doodle. "I'm afraid of Elijah."

"Pish," said Chaya Levitsky, who was thinking about all the plates of food that needed to be soaked and cleaned before bed.

"Come," said Esther Gold, rising up. She extended her hands to the boys. "All three of us will go and open the door for Elijah."

"Wonderful," said Reb Levitsky. He raised Elijah's cup, and began whispering a blessing.

The two boys followed Mrs. Gold to the door. "Now," she said, "one of you must open it."

Doodle shook his head, and David shook his.

"You do it," said one.

"No, you," said the other.

"Both of you," compromised Mrs. Gold, with a look toward heaven asking the almighty for patience.

Both boys crept to the door, put their hands on the knob, turned and pulled.

"You see," said Mrs. Gold, but her calm reassurance evaporated the instant she saw the man standing in the doorway with his hand raised about to knock again.

"Oy!"

He was a tall man, a stranger in a long dark coat. His hair was white, he had no beard, and his bushy mustache drooped down around both sides of his mouth.

"Aaaah!" shrieked young David, running back into the dining room.

"It's Elijah!" shouted Doodle, chasing after him.

Mrs. Gold, for her part, blinked twice more, and then collapsed into unconsciousness.

"Maybe he's Lebanese," said Reb Stein's voice.

Mrs. Gold's eyes fluttered open. She found herself sitting upright in a chair in the Levitsky's dining room, which was now crowded with nearly two dozen of Chelm's most prominent citizens.

"No," said Reb Kimmelman, who had traveled to the Holy Land and back. "That's not Lebanese."

Chaya Levitsky passed Esther Gold a glass of hot tea.

The stranger was sitting at the table, finishing up a bowl of matzah ball soup, as if he was starved.

"Well," said Rabbi Kibbitz, "He doesn't speak Hebrew, Yiddish, Russian or Polish. What else is there?"

Just then the visitor, who did not seem at all flustered by the attention, made a gesture that caused everyone in the room to gasp. He pretended to hold something in his hands, and then he pretended to break it apart and wipe the broken pieces inside his soup bowl.

"He wants bread?" said Reb Gold. "To sop up his soup?"

"Shouldn't Elijah know it's Pesach?" whispered Mrs. Chaipul.

"Nonsense," said Rabbi Kibbitz. "He is telling us that his broken heart has been mended by the healing power of the chicken soup."

"Mmm… Ah hah," said everyone, nodding happily, while Mrs. Levitsky kvelled with pleasure.

"If he's Elijah," said young Doodle, "does that mean the end of the world is near?"

"Hush hush," said Reb Levitsky. "Why don't you go upstairs to bed?"

"No, no," calmed Rabbi Kibbitz. "The child is asking a valid question. If it is the creator's will, Elijah will tell us in his good time."

As if he understood the Rabbi's words, the stranger pushed his plate away, mopped his face with a napkin, cleared his throat and stood.

Then he spoke. He talked for hours and hours. His eyes were bright, his hands animated, and his words were rich and filled with meaning.

The villagers of Chelm sat shoulder to shoulder in the crowded dining room, listening transfixed. The candles burned low, but still they could not look away.

Not one of them, of course, understood a single word.

Two hours later, maybe three, his voice had not faltered, but eventually it slowed and his tone lowered and quieted until the room was, at last, silent.

Still no one moved. The candles flickered. The stranger's eyes flitted around the room, expectantly. "Nu?" he seemed to say. "Nu?"

What could one say? The women and men of Chelm were known throughout the countryside as wise people. They glanced from one to another. Even Rabbi Kibbitz, the wisest of all seemed at a loss.

And then Little Doodle, who had fallen asleep on Chaya Levitsky's lap, suddenly snored—incredibly loudly for such a small boy.

"SNnHonnnk!"

The stranger's face looked utterly serious, and then his shoulders began to shudder and shake.

All of the Chelmener gasped, and wondered if they were about to witness the wrath of Elijah.

Then the stranger's odd beardless face shattered into a grin, and he began laughing loudly.

Soon, the whole house was filled with the deafening roar of laughter, which itself dissolved into the joyous songs that fill the close of every Seder. Even the stranger joined in, singing along in his foreign tongue.

The next morning the visitor was gone before anyone else awoke, and he has not yet returned.

Still, a tradition was born. If you ever see someone dozing off in classes at school, at speeches by politicians, at operas or even in Shul when the hour grows late and the sermon goes on, don't be in such a hurry to wake them. They are simply celebrating Elijah's visit to the small village of Chelm.

As it is said in the village, "To hear is human, to snore divine."

THE VILLAGE FEASTS

Cabbage Matzah

A recipe... with a story

Have you ever eaten cabbage matzah? Probably not. But in Chelm, the village of fools, they still talk about it...

Many winters ago, to battle an outburst of influenza, the villagers of Chelm used all their chickens and most of their vegetables to feed their sick neighbors in Smyrna a healing chicken soup. The Smyrnans got better, but in Chelm, all that was left was cabbage.

Because of this food shortage, the Chelmener ate cabbage for breakfast, for lunch, and for dinner. Mrs. Chaipul in her restaurant served cabbage porridge, cabbage stew, cabbage stuffed with cabbage, cabbage brisket (don't ask) and cabbage cake for dessert.

No one was happy. The children whined. The teenagers complained. The fathers groused. The mothers growled and snapped. Only Doodle, the orphan, who had an unfathomable love of cabbage, enjoyed the food. But, even young Doodle quickly learned to keep his appreciation to himself.

As spring came, mushrooms grew and wild onions flourished, the menu expanded to cabbage with mushrooms and onions. Which wasn't much better.

Reb Cantor the merchant had hoped for a delivery of supplies, but his investments were taking longer and nothing was expected to arrive until after Passover.

One morning, there was a timid knock on the door to Rabbi Kibbitz's study.

"Go away!" barked the learned man. He too was cranky from excessive consumption of cabbage.

"We've come up with a solution." Rabbi Abrahms nudged Reb Stein the baker into the room.

Rabbi Kibbitz's eyes gleamed hungrily. "Do you have rye bread?"

"No," said Reb Stein.

"Challah? Babke? Strudel?"

"Stop it!" Reb Stein cried. "You're making me hungry. No! I have invented cabbage matzah."

"Cabbage matzah?" The wise old man stared at his friend the baker. "That sounds horrible."

"It is," Reb Stein admitted. The poor baker was near tears.

"But it's kosher for Passover!" explained Rabbi Abrahms.

"But we all know, no one is going to want to buy it."

"Make it anyway," sighed Rabbi Kibbitz. "I'll pay for it out of the discretionary fund."

Reb Stein nodded glumly and returned to his bakery.

The weather was fine that year, so the villagers planned for the community Seder to be outdoors.

Mrs. Chaipul was going over the menu with her husband, Rabbi Kibbitz. (They'd gotten married, and she kept her name, but that's another story.)

"The menu," she explained, "is about what you might expect. Cabbage ball soup, chopped cabbage liver, poached cabbage, braised cabbage,

cabbage charoses, and of course Reb Stein's cabbage matzah for the meal and the afikomen."

Rabbi Kibbitz suppressed a wave of nausea. "At least we'll be outside, so we won't smell it."

No one was looking forward to Passover – except young Doodle, who offered to be a taste tester for anyone working on a new recipe.

When *Erev Pesach* arrived, everyone in Chelm trudged to the round village square to commemorate the Exodus from Egypt. With a sigh and a blessing, the service began.

The wine flowed. Reb Cantor the merchant had opened a locked cellar and rolled five barrels of "I don't know what the vintage is, but it's not cabbage" to the round village square.

When it came time to break and distribute the cabbage matzah there was rejoicing as the thick brassica wafers snapped with a resonating crack!

"This is truly the bread of affliction," Rabbi Kibbitz announced to a chorus of cheers and hoots.

Reb Stein looked doleful.

At last, after the hamotzi, everyone tasted the so-called matzah.

It was just possibly as revolting as you can imagine. Not only was the greenish cabbage matzah bitter and sour and cabbage-flavored, it was dry and stuck to the roof of your mouth and your teeth like grout on tile. The best that can be said is that no one, even the young children, spat it out.

Everyone quickly said another blessing, and gulped down another cup of wine.

But then, just before the meal was brought to the table, something happened.

Young Doodle took the opportunity to jump up onto a table and bang his glass with a spoon.

Such behavior in the middle of a Seder had never been seen! Fortunately, Doodle had been smart enough to take off his shoes and had on clean socks because Mrs. Kimmelman never would have forgiven him for getting dirty footprints on her best tablecloth.

"Excuse me," Doodle began. "I know that you all hate cabbage!"

There were cheers and boos and applause.

"But," he continued, "I look around and see my whole community gathered together, and I can't help but think how grateful I am. We have our health. We have our homes. We have each other to support us."

It is rare for the villagers of Chelm (or indeed any gathering of Jews at mealtime) to fall completely quiet, but a hush began to spread.

"We are blessed that we live in peace and freedom, and are not enslaved."

Now there was nodding and shouts of, "Amen!"

"Raise a glass with me!"

All glasses were held high.

"For this cabbage that we eat tonight," Doodle said, "represents the hope that one day all women, all men, all people will be freed from oppression and slavery."

"And freed from more cabbage!" heckled Abraham and Adam Schlemiel together.

Reb Stein the baker's eyes filled with tears, but then he began to laugh. His laughter grew louder, and it spread around the table as everyone joined in.

"May we all live in peace!" shouted Rabbi Kibbitz, who had gotten completely caught up in the moment.

Then with a rousing "Mazel Tov!" the villagers of Chelm toasted, drank, and ate with gusto.

It was only afterwards, as they got ready for bed, that Rabbi Kibbitz realized.

"You know Chanah," he told his wife. "That was one of the best Seders ever. And the food…"

The wise old man looked around to make sure no one else was listening, which considering that they were alone in their house was a certainty.

"The food," he whispered, "was delicious."

The wise old woman smiled, thought about it, nodded, and asked, "So shall I order some cabbage matzah for next year?"

"No," laughed the rabbi. "Never again!"

Home Baking Recipe for Reb Stein's Kroyt Matzah

- **Grind** one large dried cabbage very fine.
- **Stir** in just enough water so that it forms a gruel-like slurry.
- **No** salt. No yeast!
- **Spread** it thinly with a trowel on a baking sheet.
- **Bake** in a really hot oven until crisp but not black.
- **Serve** with cabbage butter, chopped cabbage livers (don't ask) and cabbage jam.
- **Enjoy** with friends and family.

The Seder Switch

"Do you know what I dreamed about last night?" Mrs. Chaipul asked her unsuspecting husband.

The chief rabbi of Chelm shook his head. "Hmm?" he asked, not yet fully awake.

"I was leading the Passover Seder," she said.

The rabbi blinked. "You were what? You were leading the Seder?"

"And what's so wrong with that?" Chanah Chaipul said. "When my first husband, Sam Klammerdinger, rest his soul, lost the power of speech, I led the Seder. Who else was going to do it?"

The rabbi sputtered, coughed, opened his mouth, and then closed it. He had remarried late in life, but after the incident of the lethal latkes had been quick to learn the first rule, "Never say anything you might regret later—no matter how right you think you are."

"Are you all right?" his wife said. "You look awful. Perhaps you should come into the restaurant for some chicken soup."

"Perhaps I will," the rabbi said. Or perhaps, he thought, I'll just go back to bed.

The rabbi had a suspicious feeling that trouble was brewing. When they were first married, Chanah had caused quite a stir when she had refused to close her restaurant or take his name. Since then, everyone in the village of Chelm assumed that she was the ruler of their house. And, if pressed, the rabbi himself might admit that held some truth.

What would they say if Chanah mentioned that she wanted to lead the Passover Seder?

Rabbi Kibbitz shuddered and tugged on his beard.

By noon the delegation appeared in the door of the Rabbi's study.

"The women all want to lead the Seder this year," Reb Cantor said.

Then they all spoke at once.

"Have you heard this nonsense?" said Reb Gold.

"It's in the Torah!" said Reb Cantor.

"I don't believe it," said Reb Kimmelman. "I traveled the world from Chelm to Palestine, and not once until today have I heard such a thing."

"Can they do it?" Reb Cantor asked.

"Never mind can they do it," interrupted Reb Gold, "should they even think about doing such a thing?"

"It's nonsense," Reb Kimmelman added. "Pure and simple."

Rabbi Kibbitz chose his next words carefully. "Why is it nonsense? True, it is traditional for the men to lead the Seder, but I have spent the morning in study and have found no law prohibiting women from taking over the role.

"But, I have an idea."

The crowded study went silent.

"If they want to lead the Seder, then it is only right that we should prepare the meal."

This suggestion produced shouts of outrage. In Chelm, and throughout the world at that time, women cooked and men worked. That was the order of things.

"Relax." Rabbi Kibbitz raised his hands to calm the assembly. "Our wives will never agree to let us take over their kitchens. Just as we feel that leading the Seder is a man's job, they also feel that making the dinner is a woman's job. How could it be otherwise?"

Ahhh! A collective sigh of relief rippled through the rabbi's study. As a group, the men thanked their leader, and hurried home to tell their wives the bargain.

Needless to say, Rabbi Kibbitz, once again was completely wrong.

One after another, the housewives of Chelm jumped at the opportunity to lead the Seder. They, led by Mrs. Chaipul, also unanimously agreed that, if the women were to lead, it was only fitting that the men put on the aprons and stir the soup.

"But, but... I don't know how to cook!" every man said to his beloved.

"Neither do I know how to lead the Seder," answered the women, "but that will not stop me."

For the next few weeks, not one man in Chelm had a kind word to say about their learned rabbi. On the streets they passed him with respectful silence. In shul they performed their duties and left quickly instead of staying afterwards for a chat with tea.

At last, Rabbi Kibbitz prayed aloud to the Almighty for assistance. But, as it has been from the time of the prophets, the King of Kings kept his silence.

So, Rabbi Kibbitz did what any man resigned to his situation does—he made the best of it. He searched through the shul's library until he found the cookbooks that his grandmother had donated, and he began making notes of recipes. Soon he was joined by one after another of the husbands, as well as some of their eldest sons.

Ordinary work in Chelm dragged to a halt as one by one the men began to prepare for this greatest of Jewish feasts. They went to the market to find the best chickens. They bought their matzah from the baker's wife, because the baker was busy chopping onions. Each worked on a dessert that they remembered from childhood, and they traded samples. They got together in a group and made a huge communal batch of chopped liver, which actually tasted pretty good. Their spirits began to rise.

At the same time, doubts began to form in the minds of the women. There was so much to remember. Did you stand up while washing your hands, or sit? Should the bitter herbs be passed to the right, or to the left? What if they did something wrong during the Seder?

But the greatest fear that the women had was similar to the men's—"What if they do their job better than me?"

At last, *Erev Pesach* arrived. The streets of Chelm grew quiet as every family gathered in a topsy-turvy home.

This night, the husbands lit the candles and the wives said the blessing over the matzah. This night the wives asked their daughters the four questions while the husbands scurried into the kitchen to check on the soup. The husbands giggled when the wives made a mistake. The wives drank all four cups of wine, while the husbands only had time to sip theirs.

At last, when the evening was done, and the Seders finished, and the dishes cleared, every man, woman and child of Chelm fell into a completely exhausted sleep.

The next day, all awoke feeling mysteriously rested. As if they all shared the same thought, they gathered in the village synagogue, which was soon as full as on the holiest of holy days.

The room quieted as Rabbi Kibbitz mounted the *bimah*. He smiled at his people and said simply, "I think we all appreciate Pesach just a little more."

Seders in Chelm were never quite the same. The communal liver chopping, for example, became something of an annual event. Most families returned to their old habits, but others, like the Kibbitz-Chaipul household, found a happy compromise.

From that Pesach on, the Rebbe and Rebbitzen together shared in the leading and in the cooking.

For, as Rabbi Kibbitz liked to say while he helped his bride wash her hands, "Is not the contribution of every person precious?"

THE VILLAGE FEASTS

By the Book

"Are they here yet?" Reb Cantor the merchant shouted as soon as he walked in the front door.

Shoshana Cantor stuck her head out of the kitchen. Her hair was frayed in disarray. Sweat was dripping from her brow. "You know, when some husbands come home they say, 'Hello. How are you? Is everything all right? How have you once again managed to prepare a Passover dinner for fifty people without the aid of additional servants? And how can I help you?'"

"You can help me by telling me whether the package with the books has arrived!" Reb Cantor retorted.

Shoshana threw a dish towel at her husband, and shouted, "One thing you had to do!"

And then she went back to work.

Reb Cantor was frantic. Over the winter, mice had gotten into the attic where they had gnawed holes and nested in his leather-bound Haggadahs. He had only discovered the destruction two months ago, when he'd gone up to put his winter coat in the cedar chest.

"It seemed good, until I dropped it," Reb Cantor told Rabbi Yohon Abrahms, the schoolteacher. They were on one of their morning walks. "The box shattered. Haggadahs were in pieces. Mice ran everywhere."

"How tragic to lose such a treasured part of your family history," Rabbi Abrahms commiserated. "Are you going to have it reprinted?

"Not a chance! I hated that book." Reb Cantor tried to catch his breath. Keeping up with the younger rabbi was always challenging. "The service was too long. Excruciating, repetitive, and boring! But because it was written by my Great-great Grandfather Izzy Cantor, every single word had to be read out loud. Whenever

I tried to skim, my wife and children said, 'No-no, you have to do it by the book.' Dinner was always cold and then after dinner it went on and on and on! Those mice did me a favor."

"So, are you canceling your Seder?" Rabbi Abrahms asked nervously.

The Cantor family Seders were famous. Every year they had out-of-town visitors, and depending on how many relatives showed up, also invited fifteen to forty villagers to enjoy one of the finest meals of their lives

"No! My wife says I have only one job this year—to replace the books." Reb Cantor stopped at the top of East Hill to rest. "I wanted to know if you would write a new Haggadah for me?"

Rabbi Abrahms smiled, "I'm flattered. I've always thought that the story of Passover could be told better…"

"I'll pay you, of course, but…" Reb Cantor held up a fat finger before the young rabbi could get into a protracted discussion of biblical minutia, "But I do have one request. My cousin Richard and his wife will be visiting from America for the holiday. His children don't speak Yiddish and don't read much Hebrew. Can you do part of it in English?"

"It will be a challenge," Rabbi Abrahms stroked his beard. "And I accept!"

For the rest of the walk back to Chelm, Rabbi Abrahms extolled at length about what was necessary - and what was unnecessary - in a Haggadah.

Four weeks later, when Reb Cantor visited Rabbi Abrahms' small house, the manuscript wasn't ready. But two weeks after that, the young rabbi finally delivered it, and Reb Cantor had immediately rushed it to the printer in Smyrna with instructions that it absolutely must be delivered before sunset on Passover. He'd even paid extra. In cash! But the books had yet to arrive.

As he dressed for the Passover dinner, Reb Cantor gnawed at his fingernails, wondering if he should send word for the other villagers to bring their own Haggadahs. That, of course, would be a chaotic mess, because no two family Haggadahs were ever alike. The best thing about Great-great Grandfather Izzy's Haggadah was that there had been fifty of them, so no one needed to share.

Now, the sun was going down. Shoshana was still in the kitchen, so Reb Cantor went to the door to begin welcoming guests.

When Rabbi Abrahms arrived, he asked, "So?"

"Not yet," Reb Cantor replied.

They both heard hoofbeats. They turned and saw a wagon clopping closer and closer down the road from Smyrna.

A smile grew across the merchant's wide face, but then fell just as quickly as he recognized Cousin Richard and his family returning from mushroom picking.

While the wagon was still rolling, before the horse had even stopped moving, Richard's two children and his wife jumped down, and ran into the house.

"My family hates me," Richard said. "It turns out that New York City mushrooms have a profoundly different effect on the digestion than those from the Black Forest."

"At least they'll recover quickly," Reb Cantor shrugged. "I only had one job this year—to get the Haggadahs for the Seder. Shoshana is going to kill me, bury me, dig me up, and then kill me again."

"Oh!" Richard said. "We stopped in Smyrna for lunch, and the printer asked me to deliver you something."

When Reb Cantor heard this, he ran to the back of the wagon.

The wooden box was tiny.

He lifted the lid.

The books inside looked small, sad and very thin.

"Did he leave out some pages?" Richard said, picking up a volume. "Great-great Grandfather Izzy's Haggadah was six times as thick."

"Isaac, the sun is down!" Shoshana Cantor shouted from inside. "If we don't start now, our guests will die of starvation!"

Reb Cantor sighed, picked up the box, and hoped for the best.

The teasing began immediately.

"Hmf. This is Rabbi Abrahms famous new Haggadah?"

"Where's the rest?"

"Who knew the schoolteacher could be so brief!"

Even Rabbi Abrahms was confused when he opened the book and saw that the English and Hebrew were written side by side. "I thought that we'd have the Hebrew pages going right to left and the English going left to right..."

But Cousin Richard's daughter Zoe and his son Jesse were feeling better. They loved being able to read the four questions in English.

And the first part of the Seder was over so quickly! It hardly seemed decent that it was already time for the meal.

Out came the matzah ball soup, the brisket and parsnips and turnips and sweet potatoes… delicious!

Everyone loved the new Haggadah, and Rabbi Abrahms was beaming from ear to ear from the compliments.

By the end of the evening, Shoshana Cantor even gave her husband a kiss on the cheek and her exhausted thanks for finishing the service before midnight.

"Listen," asked Cousin Richard, "do you think I could take a few copies back to New York? My advertising firm is working on a promotion for a coffee company. Maybe they'd like to use it."

Rabbi Abrahms shrugged, "If the coffee is good, send me a pound."

"You'll never be a businessman," said Reb Cantor, "One pound of coffee wholesale for every 100 books printed. Your company pays the shipping."

The contract was written, the deal was sealed, and now you know the story behind the world-famous Maxwell House Haggadah.

You should also know that the Abrahms-Cantor Coffee Company did very well.

Their slogan? "Good until you drop it."

THE VILLAGE FEASTS

Temptation

It was the seventh day of Passover, and Rabbi
Kibbitz was proud that he hadn't had a thought
of *chometz* in days. It was the first time in his life
that he hadn't spent every waking hour obsessing
about all the foods that he couldn't eat.

To celebrate, he'd walked to Smyrna to visit
his friend Rabbi Sarnoff and borrow a book.
After tea and matzah, the senior rabbi of Chelm
had taken his leave and his book, and began
reading as he walked home.

Now, Smyrna is a huge town, and with his nose in the book, Rabbi Kibbitz soon found himself lost. He looked up and saw he was in front of a shop, and figured he should go in and ask for directions.

He turned a page, opened the door, and was already at the counter before he realized that he had made a huge mistake.

On the seventh day of Passover, Rabbi Kibbitz of Chelm found himself standing in the middle of a bakery full to the brim with fresh goods. It smelled sooo delicious.

He was about to turn and run when a large man stepped from the back room and introduced himself in a booming voice.

"Hiya! I'm Joe DaBaker! My name is my profession. I'm from America. I travel the world collecting recipes and sharing my knowledge. Everywhere I go, I open a shop for a few months, learn something new, and then move on. This is a beautiful town here, but it's strange, I haven't had a customer all week. What can I get you?"

Rabbi Kibbitz tried to be polite. He smiled. He was afraid that if he opened his mouth, he would begin to drool.

"Can I make a suggestion?" Joe said. "I have here a Brooklyn Chocolate Cake. It's seven layers of chocolate cake with a buttercream frosting, covered with a light chocolate ganache. I'll cut you a slice."

"G-ummm," sputtered Rabbi Kibbitz. It was the most beautiful cake the wise man had ever seen.

"No cake? Hmm..." the baker shrugged. "All right. What about this? I've got a blueberry pie with a chicken-schmaltz crust. That's something I learned here. Except instead of blueberries, since they're out of season, I have found a delicious sweet squash. I can cut you a slice..."

Rabbi Kibbitz stuttered, "Well, I, um..."

"How about an Italian Canolli?" the baker persisted. "It's basically sweet riccota cheese in a crisp tube. I learned the recipe in Florence. Or, if not that, I have a linzertorte from Vienna. It's sort of an Austrian shortbread filled with raspberry jam and sprinkled with powdered sugar. Or, I know! A Hungarian mocha layer cake with rum crème filling topped with a dollop of welfenpudding, which is a sweet vanilla custard thickened with cornstarch."

At the mention of each new delight, Rabbi Kibbitz thought for a moment, and then shook his head fiercely.

"Strawberry chocolate croquembouche from Bordeaux, France? My version is a cone of choux pastry filled with chocolate and a little bit of strawberry jam, drizzled with caramel. Or a cinnamon *babka* recipe that I learned here in Smyrna. It's absolutely heavenly."

"Wait!" Joe shouted. "I know. Toll House cookies from Whitman Massachussets. A butter cookie with huge chunks of chocolate chips. They're just about done. I can bring them to you warm from the oven. Maybe you'll eat them with a little milk?"

"G-ummm.... N'a... Er..." the rabbi groaned.

"Hmm," Joe said, scratching his head. "Maybe you don't like sweets? Not a problem. What about some bread?"

The rabbi felt weak and clutched the counter for support.

Joe persisted. He reached up on a shelf and brought down an enormous round flour-dusted loaf of bread, with a square pattern cut into the top of its crust.

"I call this Italian Paesano. I baked it from a sourdough I kept alive all the way from San Francisco. Take it home. Cut the slices thick. It's perfect for dipping after a dinner of pasta and gravy, which is a kind of sauce."

Rabbi Kibbitz looked at the loaf, which was close enough to touch, but Joe didn't stop there.

He grabbed a long skinny stick of bread, and began waving it in the rabbi's face.

"This is a Parisian French baguette! It's light with a crisp crust and snowy insides. Cut it lengthwise and serve it with cheese. Or, I also have this wonderful German Black Bread. Dark as night. Thick as a leg of lamb."

With that, he gestured toward a huge lump of what Rabbi Kibbitz at first took to be a small boulder. "I've heard that the Germans smear it with schmaltzy chicken fat, which to me is kindof disgusting."

Joe DaBaker shuddered.

Rabbi Kibbitz, however, couldn't help himself, and felt a dribble of drool seep out of his mouth and drip down his chin.

"Oh, you know what?" Joe said with a wide grin. "I just learned how to tie these things." He reached into a basket and pulled out a huge Bavarian pretzel. Big pieces of salt fell from it. "I think I have some spicy mustard somewhere under the counter."

"Gaaa!" Rabbi Kibbitz said. He felt as if his knees were buckling under him.

"What about a Polish rye bread? It's dark and light swirled, with lots of caraway seeds. I have some fresh-made butter that we can smear on it... Wait, wait! I know. I finally figured it out."

Rabbi Kibbitz was startled by the sudden interruption. He stared at Joe, wondering what might possibly come next.

"You're Jewish!" Joe said, a glimmer of hope twinkling in his eye. "This is great. Just last week I got one of the bakers in Smyrna to show me how to make this."

He reached under the counter and lifted up a perfectly formed six-braided *challah*.

"This is an egg bread, right? You guys love these things for the holidays and Friday nights? This is the world's best *challah* recipe. I've got three dozen of them sitting around. I can't understand why nobody's buying them."

"Ga.gaaa.gaaa.ggaaaaah!" Rabbi Kibbitz said, stumbling back. He barely had a hold of his book as he ran out of the shop.

"What did I say?" Joe muttered to himself. "Maybe he's got one of those newfangled wheat allergies. I dunno. It's so much easier in Manhattan. At least there, they know how to make bagels."

Rabbi Kibbitz ran all the way back to Chelm. By the time he arrived at his house, it was getting dark.

"You're late," his wife, said as he panted his way into the kitchen and collapsed at the table. She handed him a glass of water. "Are you hungry?"

He couldn't speak, but he nodded his head as he drank the water.

"What would you like?" she asked.

He replied softly, "What would I like to eat?"

"It's a simple question," she said.

"Me?" the rabbi said, his voice slowly rising to a fever pitch, "I'd like cake. I'd like pie. I'd like cookies. I'd like strudel. I want bread. I want rolls. I want pretzels. I want *challah* with schmaltz! Lots and lots and lots of it."

"It's still Passover!"

"I know! I don't care. I want it all. I want it with butter and schmaltz. I want it dipped in gravy. I want it plain. I want it now!"

"All we have is matzah."

He sighed. He shrugged. "All right. I'll have some matzah."

She set a piece on the table, and jumped back as he snatched it off the plate. "Be careful you don't eat my fingers! You want some chopped liver?"

His mouth full of dry tasteless crumbs, Rabbi Kibbitz nodded, closed his eyes, and dreamed of speed-reading his way through the book so he could return it to Smyrna in only two more days…

THE VILLAGE FEASTS

Home is
Where the Seder Is

Abraham Schlemiel, his wife Rosa, and their son Abraham have moved from the village of Chelm to New York City, where they are about to celebrate their first Seder as a family...

Abraham Schlemiel stared into the empty soup bowl. He hoped that his feeling of dread wasn't showing on his face. What had he seen in *The Forward?* "Nobody can make chicken soup like a Jewish Mother." Rosa, his wife was a good cook, but she was a Gypsy. A princess of the Rom. It wasn't the same. Still, she was trying.

The small table was set with most of the elements for the Passover Seder. He'd given her a brand new *Maxwell House Haggadah,* and she'd done her best. On their best plate lay a scorched lamb bone, a pile of freshly grated horseradish, a porcelain thimble filled with salt water, a hard boiled egg, some slices of raw onion, and a mound of chopped lettuce. A stack of matzah lay on another plate beneath a beautiful red and purple scarf.

Suddenly, Abraham sneezed, barely getting his handkerchief up in time. He'd had this cold all winter.

"Bless you," Rosa said.

He smiled and looked up. Not two feet from where he sat sniffling, Rosa stood at the skinny stove, with her back to him, stirring the chicken soup. Because his nose was so stuffed, Abraham couldn't even smell the soup, which, he decided, might not be a bad thing.

Their apartment was so small. Young Abraham, their son, was dozing in the bathtub on the other side of the table. Not that he was so little any more. Twelve years old. Abraham smiled at the sleeping boy, feeling badly that they couldn't afford a decent bed.

Every morning Young Abraham was up at dawn selling newspapers to the bankers on Wall Street. Then he went to school, and after that there were the preparations for his *bar mitzvah*, plus the violin practice that his mother insisted on.

Abraham, the father, had offered to cook the Passover dinner. His job was working as a chef at Fraunces Tavern, the oldest restaurant in New York City, on Pearl Street near the tip of Manhattan. He was proud of his job. Built in 1762, the restaurant was famous for the farewell banquet that George Washington gave for his officers in 1783 after the Revolutionary War.

It was somewhat ironic, Abraham knew, a Jew cooking in a *treif* establishment, but he managed. He brought his own lunches and asked his helpers to taste the food for him. The joke was that in Abraham Schlemiel's kitchen, the dishwashers ate better than he did.

"No," Rosa had said. "I'll cook. Your Passover is a day for tradition. The tradition is that the wife cooks, and the husband leads the, what do you call it, Saber?"

"Seder," he corrected.

Abraham thought about explaining the new tradition in Chelm of men and women sharing the preparations, but decided to take a different approach.

"Rosa, after a long day of sewing shirts in the factory, why do you want to do everything yourself? I'd be happy to help."

"You cook all day," she said, firmly. "Besides there's not so much to do."

Abraham blinked. He remembered his mother and grandmother and his baby sister, Shemini, scurrying around the kitchen for weeks in preparation for the Seder.

Abraham missed home. He missed Chelm in the springtime with its muddy streets.

The streets of New York weren't paved with gold. You found that out pretty quickly after you arrived. The cobblestone streets were filled with holes, and filthy from horses. And the sidewalks were filthy from dogs. Nobody cleaned up.

At least in Chelm the worst you would do is fill your boots with mud. He missed the shul, and the rabbis, and the constant gossip and the discussions in Yiddish, Polish and Russian. The languages on Orchard Street were familiar, but the work was so different. In New York City, there were no farmers, no craftsmen, only factories and shopkeepers and pushcarts. And everything was so crowded.

Most of all he missed his family. His father, mother, sister and of course his brother, Adam. They were twins—they were "the twins." How could they not miss each other? For a moment, Abraham tried reaching out with his mind, trying to send his thoughts out across the ocean and a continent to his brother. But... Nothing. No answer. It was too far, or Adam was asleep, or not listening.

"Papa Abraham? Little Abe," Rosa announced. "It's time."

Young Abraham sat up, yawned, climbed out of his bathtub, stretched, and sat down at the table.

As befitted the head of the household, Abraham, the father, began reading from the *Haggadah*.

Rosa lit the candles. She helped her husband wash his hands. She listened carefully as he told her the story of the Exodus from Egypt.

They both beamed as their son read the four questions perfectly.

As Abraham sped through the service, he remembered the battles that he and Adam had fought over who was the youngest, who would have the honor of reading the questions. He missed his grandparents, who always made jokes. And his father, who always sang so badly off key that everyone else's voice sounded good.

At last it was time for dinner, the moment that Abraham had been dreading.

Rosa brought the heavy soup pot to the table, which shuddered under its weight.

"Before you eat," she said, sitting down. "I have to apologize. This soup is all we have. I wanted to make the *kiggel* and *kugel* and *giggle*, or whatever else you call what you're used to eating. I was going to roast a brisket. But there was a fire at another factory, and the girls' families needed some money to help with the hospital bills. So, I gave away what we had, and kept just enough for the soup. I'm so sorry."

Young Abraham's face fell.

Abraham, the father and husband, shook his head and smiled. "Rosa, no. No. You did well. We share what we have. Thank you."

Amazing how much he loved them both after all these years.

Their son tried hard not to look disappointed.

"Don't worry," she told him, "We've got plenty of matzah balls, and I saved out some chicken from the pot so that it wouldn't taste like rubber."

Rosa lifted the lid of her grandmother's pot, and ladled out portions into each of their bowls.

Abraham braced himself, hoping for the best. Whether it was too salty or too weak or too vinegary or too peppery, he promised himself he would say nothing. If the matzah balls were rock hard like Mrs. Chaipul's, crumbly to bits, or raw in the middle, he would keep his mouth shut. His face would remain neutral, and then he would feign joy and delight.

Finally, his spoon dipped down into the rich golden broth. He brought it to his lips, and slurped.

The moment he swallowed, his nose cleared, and for the first time in weeks he could smell.

He smelled the soup! The rich aroma filled his nose, the warm taste filled his mouth, and his face broke into a grin. The miracle of chicken soup.

He paused, allowing for another moment of hope, and then steeled himself as he stared at the floating matzah balls.

Tentatively he cut into a knaidel. It broke cleanly. He raised it to his lips and chewed. Not that he had to chew very hard. Firm, yet light, Rosa's matzah ball was filled with a hearty flavor that was indescribable.

"Well?" Rosa said, nervously waiting for the verdict.

"Delicious," Abraham said. "Perfect.

Abraham reached over and took his wife's left hand and his son's right hand. "Rosa, Abraham. This is home. We need nothing more than each other, but if we are allowed only one thing to eat, I certainly hope it is this soup."

Rosa glowed.

"Mama, can I have some more?" Young Abraham said. His bowl was empty.

Everyone laughed. And the small family lived happily in their cramped apartment, until they moved to the suburbs. But that, as they say, is another story.

The Village Will
Not Go Hungry

Two weeks before Pesach, Rabbi Yohon Abrahms and his Yeshiva students were discussing Passover preparations. A lively debate had arisen over the definition of leavened bread...

"I still don't understand why we can't use yeast," said Joel Cantor. "In Exodus it just says that the bread didn't have time to rise."

"They didn't know about yeast in those days," said Jacob Stein, the baker's son, who knew the complete history of bread. "They just left the bread out and waited for it to rise, because the yeast was floating in the air."

Rabbi Abrahms was pleased at his student's enthusiasm. He tugged on his beard, and said, "Tell me, David, what do you think?"

David Gold, the son of the cobbler, didn't answer. He stood up and fled from the room.

"What did I say?" Rabbi Abrahms asked the rest of his students.

Joel Cantor raised his hand. "The Golds are not eating matzah this year."

Rabbi Abrahms was shocked, "What? Why?"

Joel Cantor said, "It's too expensive."

"It is not!" Jacob Stein said, defending his father's bakery, which was known for its delicious matzah.

"They still can't afford it," said the quiet voice of Rachel Cohen, the daughter of the tailor, and the first girl to be admitted to the Yeshiva.

"Hmm," Rabbi Abrahms stroked his beard thoughtfully. "Perhaps we should discuss *tsedaka*, charity…"

Later that evening, the Village Council of Elders summoned Reb Gold to the Synagogue's meeting hall. Behind the long table sat Rabbi

Kibbitz, Reb Cantor the Merchant and Reb Stein the Baker.

Reb Gold stood before them with his hat held in his hand, and his head bare except for his kippah.

"Joshua," Rabbi Kibbitz began, "we are sorry to bring you here like this."

"What do you mean, you're not going to buy my matzah!" snapped Reb Stein.

"Sha, sha," Rabbi Kibbitz raised his hand. "This is an inquiry, not an inquisition."

Reb Gold looked at the floor and spoke in a quiet voice, "I'm sorry, but We have no money for matzah."

"Then I'll give you some matzah," barked Reb Stein. "When you get some money, you'll give me what you can."

"No one buys shoes from me any more," Reb Gold said plainly. "Not since the shoe factory in Smyrna was built. Shoes from there cost less than my materials alone."

The elders shifted uncomfortably. Every single one of them was wearing a pair of shoes from that factory.

"But you can still repair shoes, can't you?" asked Reb Cantor.

"Why?" replied Reb Gold." Are your shoes worn out?"

"Not yet," Reb Cantor admitted.

Reb Gold shrugged. "I would never be able to repay Reb Stein for the matzah. We have a large bag of rice in the cellar. My family will eat that until after Passover."

"Rice? Rice?" bellowed Reb Stein. "Nonsense! You will eat my matzah!"

"Quiet. Settle down," Rabbi Kibbitz commanded.

Reb Stein fell silent.

"It is common," the rabbi continued, "for the village of Chelm to take care of its citizens."

"I cannot accept charity forever," Reb Gold said.

"Then what will you do when you run out of rice?" asked Reb Cantor.

Reb Gold looked down at his shoes. They were well made shoes, beautifully crafted. His father had taught him how to make shoes, like his grandfather and his great grandfather. Perhaps they were not as stylish as those from the factory, but they would last for years—for decades. He had gone so far as to visit the factory in Smyrna to ask for a job, even though it was a three hour walk in each direction. The factory owner had shown him how the shoes were made. Each man in the factory worked on just one part of the shoe—the sole, the heel, the cuff, the tongue.

The owner offered Reb Gold the job of punching eyelets. That would be it, day in and day out—punching eyelets—not even threading the laces! Reb Gold was a craftsman, not a machine. He had graciously refused the job, and walked sadly back to Chelm.

"Have you any family?" asked Rabbi Kibbitz.

"Does he have family?" Reb Stein laughed, "They visit all the time! From all over Russia and Poland. Even from as far away as England. They come into my shop and marvel at the *challah*."

"They come into my store," agreed Reb Cantor, "and they always buy something for souvenirs."

"I will not become a beggar and impose upon my family!" cried Reb Gold, who was nearly in tears. "I will not take my family away and leave our home. Chelm is the most beautiful place in the world! Our streets are well kept. Our round village square is a mystery. The trees bloom with pink flowers in the spring and then the leaves turn brilliant in autumn. The water is pure, and the mind of everyone who lives here is bright with wonder and astonishment.

"If I leave the village, I know everyone will say, 'Look, there goes Joshua Gold. He was too stupid to stay in Chelm!'"

The poor cobbler fell silent, and rather than look at his shoes, he closed his eyes.

Reb Cantor, on the other hand, was smiling. He laughed. "I have an idea!"

"What is a *travel agent*?" Esther Gold asked her husband when he returned home that evening.

"I will bring visitors to Chelm!" Joshua Gold answered with excitement. "I will organize tours. You don't even have to be Jewish to enjoy the village. People will come from far and wide to our little village, and when they go they will take lots of souvenirs and presents, and a little bit of the wisdom of Chelm home with them."

"Does it pay?" Esther asked, not daring to hope.

"Enough. I'll also make shoes," Joshua answered, patting his wife's hand. "To begin I will work for Reb Cantor. When the tourists arrive, I will receive a commission."

"All this for talking and getting people to come and visit us?" She rolled her eyes. "What will they think of next?"

"Maybe we could open a hotel?" suggested young David.

Reb Gold smiled at his son. "Thank you, David, for sharing our burden. Without you, and the help of the others, this would have been a very difficult year."

With that, the small family gathered together, and hugged each other with joy.

Was Reb Gold successful? Of course he was.

My friends, that is why the story of the small village of Chelm is told far and wide, even to the ends of the planet.

The End

Author's Note

These tales of *The Village Life* are fiction. Although the villagers are Jewish, the stories are meant for readers and listeners of all ages, backgrounds and beliefs. Traditional in feel and inspired by the past, they are meant to be contemporary and timeless, and to bring people together across boundaries.

But in what order should they be read?

Time in the village is not always linear, and lives intertwine. This may lead to some confusion. Which is natural, given the nature of Chelm, and the fact that some stories were written decades before others.

The seasonal holiday collections can be enjoyed alone or shared within families, while the novels, especially

The Village Twins and *The Council of Wise Women*, are fare for older readers.

Several chapters from *A Village Romance* also appear in *Winter Blessings* and *The Village Feasts*. I hope you'll forgive the repetition, because stories taste different in different contexts.

As Rabbi Kibbitz often says at dinnertime, "The brisket is tender. The kasha is toothsome. The gravy is good. Together, they are delicious."

To which Mrs. Chaipul raises an eyebrow and answers, "If you want more, just ask."

– *Izzy Abrahmson, Providence*

A Village Glossary

Yiddish is a language of sound and subtlety. Hebrew is an ancient tongue. This is a Chelmenish interpretation of words that you may, or may not know.

Chelm: The Village. The place where most of the people in this book live. A traditional source of Jewish humor. The "ch" in Chelm (and most Yiddish and Hebrew transliteration) is pronounced like you've got something stuck in your throat. "Ch-elm."

Chelmener: the people who live in The Village. Often known as the wisefolk of Chelm. Sometimes called Chelmites. Sometimes called, "The Fools of Chelm".

babka: a delicious cake. Usually served with coffee, tea and gossip.

bar mitzvah: the Jewish coming-of-age ceremony for boys. Celebrated at 13. Almost always catered.

bat or bas mitsvah: the coming of age ceremony for girls. They actually didn't do this in Chelm, until Rachel Cohen. But that's not a Passover story.

bimah: the platform at the front of the synagogue where the rabbi stands so that everyone can hear him.

Cantor: a person who leads a religious service with song. Neither Rabbi Kibbitz nor Rabbi Yohon Abrahms were very good singers, but the village budget wasn't large enough to hire a cantor. Not to be confused with Reb Cantor the merchant.

challah: a braided egg bread. In English, the plural of challah is challah. Challah is **not** eaten during Passover.

Chanukah: the festival of lights. Celebrated in the winter, Chanukah commemorates the victory of the Maccabees over King Antiochus. The miracle of Chanukah was that one day's measure of oil burned in the Temple for eight days. Sometimes spelled Hanukkah. Or Hanukah.

chometz: all sorts of delicious baked goods that aren't kosher for passover. Only obsessed about during Passover.

dreidel: a four-sided top spun in a children's game during Chanukah. Although sometimes played for money, Dreidel is usually played for high stakes, like raisins and nuts.

Erev: the evening that begins a holiday. Jewish holidays start at sunset and end after sunset.

goyishe: someone or something that is not Jewish.

goob: when something is so delicious that you can't pronounce the letter "d" because you're too busy eating, it's "goob."

hamotzi: blessing over the bread—or the matzah.

kabalah: Jewish mysticism, often numerological. It's secret: shhh!

kiggel (or kugel): a pudding. Sometimes savory. Sometimes sweet. Mmmm.

knaidel: a matzah ball dumpling served in chicken soup. Often served during Passover. The plural of knaidel is knaidlach.

kreplach: a dumpling. Jewish wontons. Tasty! But not kosher for Passover.

kvell: to glow with pride.

latke: a pancake fried in oil. At Passover, latkes are made with matzah meal. At Hanukkah they are made with potatoes.

matzah: unleavened bread made from flour and water with no salt or yeast. Sometimes spelled "matzoh." You can eat matzah year round, but you must eat matzah during Passover, the holiday celebrating the Israelites' exodus from Egypt. Also known as the bread of affliction, perhaps because it is tasteless, bland and binding.

matzah brie: fried matzah. Break crisp matzah into pieces. Moisten it. Dump out the water. Mix it with eggs and salt, and fry it to make matzah brie. Yum!

mishugas: craziness. Normal in Chelm.

mitzvah: a commandment, often a good deed. Not to be confused with a Bar Mitzvah, which is the coming of age ceremony for boys.

mashgiach - the rabbi in charge of making sure everything's kosher.

mensch: a good guy. A nice fellah. Kind and generous. You want your daughter to marry one.

nigun: a melody or tune whose words have no meaning. Perfect for Chelmener!

nosh: Food or snacking. You can nosh, or you can have a nosh, but you don't nosh a nosh.

nu: What? No, really. What!? Nu? You understand?

oy: an expression of excitement and often pain. "Oy! My back!" or "Oy, I can't believe you're wearing that to a wedding!"

Passover/Pesach: the celebration of the Exodus from Egypt. Celebrated for eight days in the diaspora or seven days, depending on where you live and what you believe.

plotz: to explode. As in, "I ate so much matzah brie I nearly plotzed."

Rabbi: a scholar, a teacher, a leader in the community.

Reb: a wise man. And, since everyone in Chelm is wise, the men are all called Reb... as in Reb Stein, Reb Cantor, and so on. (Yes, of course there are wise women in Chelm! They just don't brag about it.)

Seder: the Passover feast. A huge meal with lots of prayers, songs and stories. No leavened bread. No challah. Just matzah. Followed by seemingly endless days of matzah. Oy.

Shabbas: the Jewish Sabbath. Starts Friday at sundown and ends Saturday after sunset. Sometimes called Shabbat or Shabbos.

shmear: a big hunk of cream cheese usually spread on a bagel, but during Passover it is permissible to shmear matzah. Just be careful so you don't break it.

Shmura Matzah: a special matzah made from carefully guarded wheat. Often round. Often burned. Don't use it for matzah brie.

Smyrna: the nearest town to Chelm.

schmaltz: chicken fat. Used in cooking and spread on bread. Source of many heart attacks.

shmootz, shmuts: dust, dirt, those little brown flecks of stuff that you find here and there.

Shul: the synagogue.

Torah: The Five Books of Moses. The first five books of the Hebrew Bible, which is frequently called the Old Testament.

tsedaka: a gift of charity.

tuchas: the posterior.

yad: a pointer. You're not supposed to touch the Torah Scroll as you read, so instead of pointing with your finger, you use a yad. The word means hand, so it often looks like a tiny hand with its index finger outstretched.

yenta: a gossip, a busybody.

yeshiva: the religious school. In Chelm, the yeshiva is the only school.

Yom Kippur: The Day of Atonement. No one eats or drinks. No kiggle, knaidel, babke, challah, or shmaltz or even matzah. Always followed by the break-fast, a sumptuous meal served after dark. All the food at the break-fast is eaten in a matter of moments.

zaftig: plump, but in a good way. Rubenesque.

About the Author

Izzy Abrahmson is the pen name for Mark Binder, a professional storyteller, and the author of more than two dozen books and audio books for families and adults. He has toured the world delighting readers and listeners of all ages with his stories, interspersed with his unique klezmer harmonica sounds.

Under his "real" name, Mark began writing about The Village as the editor of *The Rhode Island Jewish Herald*. These stories were so popular that they have been published in newspapers and magazines around the world. His epic *Loki Ragnarok* was nominated for an Audie Audiobook Award for Best Original Work, and *Transmit Joy* won a Parents' Choice Gold Award for Audio Storytelling. Mark is also a playwright, and the founder of the American Story Theater. In his spare time he bakes bread and makes pizza. He lives in Providence with his wife, who is a brilliant ceramic artist.

For tour dates, news, and bonus material visit:
izzyabe.com or **markbinderbooks.com**

Thank you

We hope you've enjoyed this book.

May we send you a bonus story as a gift?
Send an email to:
villagefeasts@izzyabe.com

Please do consider telling your friends
and writing a review.

You can also tag us on social media
#TheVillageLife
@IzzyAbrahmson

We value your readership.
Have an excellent day.

The Village Life Series

"The Village is snuggled in an indeterminate past that never was but certainly should have been, a past filled with love, humor, adventures and more than occasional misadventures. And when you go, be sure to bring the kids." – *The Times of Israel*

Winter Blessings

National Jewish Book Award for Family Literature Finalist!
Eleven funny and heart-warming Chanukah stories and a novella.

"Parents and grandparents will enjoy reading selections aloud and retelling the stories." – *AJL Newsletter*

The Village Feasts

Ten tasty Passover tales for adults and children of all ages. Delightful and amusing.

The Village Twins - a novel for adults

When the seventh daughter of a seventh daughter has twins, you know there will be trouble. Abraham and Adam Schlemiel star in this warm comedy that blends ordinary life with adventure and epic confusion.

"In the spirit of Sholem Aleichem… identical twins, confused from birth, will charm with their simplicity and sincerity." – *AudioFile*

A Village Romance - a novella

He's the wisest man in the village. She runs the only restaurant. They are both widowed…. What could possibly go wrong?

"engaging tales… Village stories that deftly lift a curtain on a world of friendly humor and touching details of Jewish life."
– *Kirkus Reviews*

The Council of Wise Women - a novel for adults – Coming Soon!

Another set of twins? Oy! The birth of Rachel and Yakov Cohen bring new blessings and challenges to The Village.

books, ebooks, and audiobooks available at your favorite retailer and at IzzyAbe.com

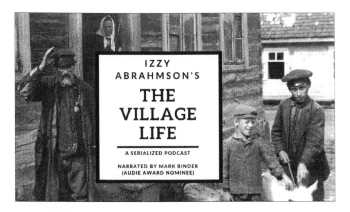

The Village Life Podcast

Welcome to The Village!

On the edge of The Black Forest, somewhere between Russia and Poland (and occasionally Germany) is a small community. Eighty or so houses, more chickens than people. Think Mayberry or Lake Woebegon, except Jewish.

You'll meet the men, women and children who live and work here. You'll laugh at their misadventures, and smile as problems resolve.

As Reb Gold says, "Visiting the Village is like eating warm rye bread. You don't need to be Jewish to enjoy it."

New episodes drop every week or so.

Find Izzy Abrahmson's Village Life Podcast on Apple, Spotify, Google and more

**Get in touch via email:
info@lightpublications.com**

Made in the USA
Middletown, DE
04 February 2022

59492997R00064